Alexandra and the Vanishing Unicorns

by Margaret Holland and Craig B. McKee
illustrated by Estella Lee Hickman

Willowisp Press

Published by Willowisp Press, Inc.
401 E. Wilson Bridge Road, Worthington, Ohio 43085

Copyright ©1986 by Willowisp Press, Inc.

Printed in the United States of America

10 9 8 7 6 5 4 3 2 1

ISBN 0-87406-089-3

Alexandra was playing in the forest with the other unicorns. Her crystal horn sparkled in the sunlight. Suddenly, she noticed that two of her friends had disappeared. There were only four other unicorns where there had been six.

Were they playing hide-and-seek? she wondered. She searched all their favorite hiding places. But two unicorns were still missing.

The next day when
Alexandra went to
play, there were only
two other unicorns.

The following day, no other unicorns appeared. Where were all the others? Alexandra wondered. She couldn't understand where her friends had gone.

Alexandra asked the trees and rocks and squirrels and birds. But none of them had seen the missing unicorns.

Alexandra was worried. She decided to visit her old friend Ursula, the wisest of all the unicorns. She found Ursula deep in the forest. Ursula was standing on her rock looking tired and sad.

"My friends have disappeared," said Alexandra. "I can't find any of them. And the trees and rocks and squirrels and birds haven't seen them either."

"I knew something was wrong," sighed Ursula. "But even when I tuned my horn to the four directions, I could not tell what was happening. And now the unicorns are vanishing."

As she spoke, Ursula herself began to fade away. Just as she disappeared, Ursula whispered, "Only you can help, Alexandra...."

Alexandra was
terrified. What can I
do? What can be
happening to all the
unicorns? she wondered.

Then she had an idea.
She would go to her
friend Grandfather
Tree for help.

Alexandra flew straight to Grandfather Tree and told him what had happened. Grandfather Tree sent out a rustle among all the trees in the forest. But the trees answered back that there were no other unicorns anywhere in the forest.

"You are the only
unicorn left, Alexandra,"
said Grandfather Tree.
"And I don't know why
only you are left.
Perhaps you should
leave the forest before
you too disappear."

"But where can I go?"
sighed Alexandra.

"Why don't you go to Crystal Valley?
Perhaps the Great Crystal who helped you find
your horn can help you again."

Alexandra nodded. She waved good-bye to Grandfather Tree and flew off. All night long she flew, following the North Star straight to Crystal Valley.

Just as the stars began to fade, Alexandra saw Crystal Valley ahead. Soon she stood in front of the Great Crystal.

"Oh, Great Crystal, I have come again to ask your help. The unicorns are disappearing, and no one knows where to find them. I am the only one left. Can you help me?"

"I will try," replied the Great Crystal. And with that, the Great Crystal sent out a powerful beam of light.

The Great Crystal's light scanned
in all directions. "That's very strange,"
the Great Crystal said. "The unicorns
still exist, but they have faded. They
are vanishing into the Land of
Make-Believe."

"How can that be?" asked Alexandra.
"I'm still here."

"Only your crystal horn has kept you here," said the Great Crystal.

"But why is this happening?" asked Alexandra.

She began to cry. And as her tears touched the ground, they turned into flowers.

"Whenever one child stops believing in unicorns, a unicorn will vanish and become trapped in the Land of Make-Believe."

"Isn't there anything we can do to keep the unicorns from disappearing?" asked Alexandra.

"The children of the world hold the key," explained the Great Crystal.

"Crystals can help the children believe again. We have always been here to help people see the wonders of the world around them," the Great Crystal said.

"Then why don't you go to the children?" asked Alexandra.

"Alas! We have no way to get there," said one of the smaller crystals.

"I could fly you there," said Alexandra.

"No, you don't understand," said another of the smaller crystals. "If you went there, you too would disappear."

"There is a chance, Alexandra," said the Great Crystal. "If you go at night while the children are asleep, you can leave crystals under their pillows. Then they might begin to dream of unicorns. And they might begin to remember."

"But you must be careful," said the Great Crystal. "You must return before the children wake up, or you too will vanish into the Land of Make-Believe. Even your crystal horn cannot protect you."

"I promise to return in time," said Alexandra.

At that, Alexandra saw many of the crystals lighting up. As she walked through the valley, the brightest crystals clung to her.

Soon Alexandra was covered with crystals. That night, Alexandra left Crystal Valley.

Soon she was flying over the houses of the children. The crystals dropped one by one to rest under the pillows of children everywhere.

Alexandra flew and flew. She flew over houses covered with snow and houses surrounded by palm trees. She flew until all but the last crystal had dropped to earth.

Suddenly she noticed that the stars were
beginning to fade.

I must finish, thought Alexandra.

But just then, she saw a child staring
up at the sky. Alexandra
felt herself beginning
to fade away.

As she was about to
disappear, Alexandra saw
the last crystal land
in the child's hand.

The child went back to bed. He put the crystal under his pillow and began to dream of unicorns. And Alexandra flew home.

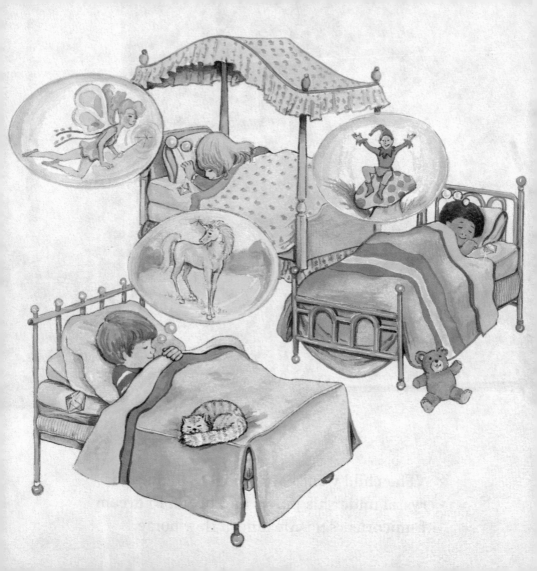

The crystals helped the children dream.
They helped them dream of unicorns
and elves and fairies and all the wonders
that children can dream of.

And because the children's dreams were true, the unicorns returned to the forest.